P9-CSA-459

The Improbable Cat

ALLAN AHLBERG

The Improbable Cat

Illustrated by Peter Bailey

DELACORTE PRESS

PALATINE PUBLIC LIBRARY DISTRICT
700 N. NORTH COURT
PALATINE, ILLINOIS 60067-8159

Published by
Delacorte Press
an imprint of
Random House Children's Books
a division of Random House, Inc.
New York

Text copyright © 2002 by Allan Ahlberg
Illustrations copyright © 2002 by Peter Bailey

Originally published in Great Britain in 2002 by Penguin Books

All rights reserved. No part of this book may be reproduced or
transmitted in any form or by any means, electronic or mechanical,
including photocopying, recording, or by any information storage
and retrieval system, without the written permission of the
publisher, except where permitted by law.

The trademark Delacorte Press is registered in the U.S. Patent
and Trademark Office and in other countries.

Visit us on the Web! www.randomhouse.com/kids
Educators and librarians, for a variety of teaching tools, visit us at
www.randomhouse.com/teachers

LIBRARY OF CONGRESS CATALOGING-IN-PUBLICATION DATA

Ahlberg, Allan.
The improbable cat / Allan Ahlberg ; illustrated by Peter Bailey.
p. cm.
Summary: A strange creature, which initially looks like a cat,
appears in the yard of Davy's house one day and proceeds to
destroy his family's life by "hypnotizing" everyone but Davy and
his little brother.
ISBN 0-385-73186-8
[1. Monsters—Fiction. 2. Animals—Fiction. 3. Horror stories.]
I. Bailey, Peter, ill. II. Title.
PZ7.A2688Im 2004
[Fic]—dc22
2003055654

The text of this book is set in 11-point Cochin.
Printed in China
August 2004
10 9 8 7 6 5 4 3 2 1

Also by Allan Ahlberg

Novels and Stories
The Clothes Horse
It Was a Dark and Stormy Night
Jeremiah in the Dark Woods
My Brother's Ghost · Ten in a Bed
The Man Who Wore All His Clothes
The Woman Who Won Things

Picture Books
The Adventures of Bert · A Bit More Bert
Each Peach Pear Plum
The Jolly Postman · The Jolly Christmas Postman
The Jolly Pocket Postman · Starting School
The Bravest Ever Bear · The Cat Who Got Away
Monkey Do! · Peek-A-Boo
The Snail House · Treasure Hunt

Contents

I have wanted (and not *wanted) to tell this story for a while—for years, really. Get it off my chest, as you might say. But I never did. And the reason is (I have lately come to realize), the reason is . . . I* didn't know it. *I mean, I couldn't tell it all; there was one bit missing. Y'see, something happens in this story that I can't account for. Something crazy—impossible—horrific. And there really is no explanation, none I can think of anyway. No dark lord or magic wardrobe, for instance; no mad scientist either. Nothing like that, it just . . . happened.*

There again, as I get older (I'm at university now), I begin to think, well, what's normal anyway? What's ordinary? Is a boiled egg ordinary, a mobile phone—a planet? I can remember years ago we did this project on probability in Mrs. Miller's class. For five minutes in pairs (George and I were a pair) we tossed coins and recorded how they fell: heads, tails, tails, heads.

Toward the end there was a commotion. A couple of girls were leaping about and yelling, "Look, Miss!" There on the floor, their coin between the boards was stood on end. They had cheated, of course, but that's it, isn't it—or it could be. I mean, for instance, most kittens become cats (if they live long enough), don't they? The odds on a kitten not becoming a cat are huge, but not impossible maybe. Sometimes . . . sometimes, unaided, the coin will stand on end.

So here we go. My name is David Burrell and when this story begins (I think I can tell it now) I am twelve years old and getting on with my life, alive and kicking . . . in the ordinary world.

1

How It Started

M Y FAMILY WERE A soft lot, Dad included. They hardly knew what hit them. There they all were that summer's afternoon clearing up after Josie's party. Mum and Dad carrying leftovers back into the house, Josie collecting paper plates, Luke half-asleep in his bouncer.

All of a sudden, the prettiest little smoky-gray kitten that any of them had ever seen came *limping* out of the hedge and stood miaowing before them. Like a bunch of sheep—"Ah!"—the three of them went rushing forward. Even Lukey bounced into life. Yes, that little cat had captured their attention right enough. Fact is, they were in love with it in an instant.

Anyway, that was how it started. There was the cat, there was my besotted family, and there was I at my bedroom window, watching it all. I had retreated hours earlier to escape a houseful of screaming seven-year-old girls. Billy was beside me, dozing on the bed, yet ready for a walk if one was offered.

When I came down later, Dad was still in the garden. Mum and Josie had the kitten between them on the sofa. They did not look up as I entered the room. A fast-asleep Lukey was lolling unnoticed in his carrycot. Out in the kitchen a pan of baby food was simmering itself dry on the hob. There was a hint of burning in the air.

In the next day or so we made efforts to find the owner of this kitten. Dad knocked on a few doors. Mum and Josie put a postcard in the newsagent's window. I asked around. Nothing. This kitten was entirely unconnected, had popped up out of nowhere, was nobody's. Only now, of course, he was ours.

It was August, halfway through the

summer holidays. Dad left for work each day; he was a librarian. Mum was a teacher. She and Josie spent much of their time making a banner for the Ban the Lorries campaign. These huge things, juggernauts really, were using Crompton Street and Cavendish Road as a cut-through to the motorway. There was a protest planned for this coming Saturday.

Meanwhile, the kitten was continuing to infiltrate our lives, wanting ever to be made a fuss of, wanting ever to be fed. Food. I didn't notice it at first, but Mum wasn't buying any of the usual brands of cat food. No, it was more like sardines and pilchards, salmon even. Salmon—for a cat!

Truth is, I was keeping clear of this animal. I was allergic to cats, well, some of them. Nothing serious, just sneezing and that sort of thing. Besides, it *was* the holidays, the sun was out and George and I had stuff to do. So it was a little while before I realized just how well this kitten was thriving on his deluxe diet.

It was the Saturday. The Ban the Lorries banner was propped up in the hall. Mum was yelling instructions to Josie from upstairs, to brush her hair, put her shoes on, and so on. Josie made no reply and eventually I got involved.

Josie was in the sitting room on the sofa, the kitten stretched out across her lap having its ears rubbed. "Kitten"—it was bigger than Billy! (How could I not have noticed?) It gave me a look as I put my head round the door. Josie ignored me.

Her face was flushed, her eyes heavy and glazed, which was the state she often got into when watching TV. But the TV was off.

2

Billy

BILLY WAS A MONGREL terrier, brown and white, about four years old. He was the boldest little dog, afraid of nothing. I have known him see off an Alsatian. Cats, however, he mostly ignored. With the kitten it was different.

They encountered each other that first evening in the kitchen. Billy instantly went

rigid, y'know, like a wooden dog. The fur along his back stood on end, a growl formed in his throat. My mother in alarm scooped up the kitten, while Dad dragged Billy back into the garden. He stayed there for some time, pawing at the French windows, growling and peering, anxiously it seemed, into the room. The kitten was not bothered at all.

That Saturday, while Mum and Josie were out protesting, I went round to George's and spent most of the day there. George lived with his mum; they had this big house, which his mum used mainly as an animal refuge. She had everything in there: hedgehogs, tortoises—swans even. There was a paddock at the side of the house with pens, hutches and various other shelters in it. Three or four elderly donkeys grazed there, and a small horse.

George and I did jobs for his mum, feeding the animals mostly. We swung around on his tire-on-a-rope for a while and threw sticks in the river for the dogs. At lunchtime I talked to George's mum about the kitten.

"The thing is, Alma, how fast do kittens grow?"

"Pretty fast," said Alma. "More hum-mus?"

"How fast in a week?"

"Well . . ."

"See, this kitten — I think it's doubled in size, tripled even."

"Unlikely," said George.

"No, really."

"Perhaps it's got some kind of eating disorder," said Alma.

Then George's gran (Alma's mother) arrived, and she joined in. "What are you feeding it on?"

"Salmon."

"*Salmon*—ha, no wonder."

After that the conversation shifted somehow into fantasy—jokes mainly—about an almost spherical cat that Joyce had once owned, overweight stick insects and, finally, dieting. Alma had merely to look at a profiterole, she said, to put on the pounds. Joyce had merely to read the recipe.

On Sunday I slept in late, only to be woken at about ten o'clock by a loud crash, and shouting and barking. I rushed downstairs.

Mum, in her dressing gown, was swatting at Billy with a rolled-up newspaper. Dad was trying to grab him as he darted about. The kitten, unperturbed, was up on the table, a shattered jug all over the floor. Billy was going berserk.

By half-past ten his bed had been moved out into the garage, together with his bowls, his ball and anything else he possessed. Billy was banished.

3

The Landing

LOOKING BACK, IT'S HARD to be sure now when my earliest suspicions arose. (Billy's instincts, of course, were another matter. If only dogs could talk, none of this would have happened.) One thing I do know, it wasn't just the size, the growing. Even from the start I must have sensed something was wrong. I mean, take that first evening: a limping kitten, which once it got into the house never limped again, and after a day or so never miaowed again either. Or purred. Or, as far as I could see, even washed itself.

I tried talking to Dad.

"But who started it? What did he do?"

We were in the garage, clearing a space for Billy's bed.

"Billy started it—give me a hand with this." The garage was crammed with bikes and jumble-sale stuff. "Turned really savage. I've never seen him like that."

Out in the garden, tied up to the mower, Billy looked calm enough.

"It's just for a while," said Dad. He brushed a cobweb from his hair. "Till things settle down."

I felt really angry then, indignant on Billy's behalf. "But it's Billy's *house*, Dad—

Billy comes first. Put the cat in the garage."

"It's only a kitten, Davy."

"It doesn't look like a kitten—look at the size of it." In my frustration, I kicked out at a sack of compost. "That's another thing—*why is it getting so big?*"

Dad removed his glasses and rubbed his eyes. I could see now the darker shadows around them. "Maybe it's the breed," he said.

In the afternoon I took Billy up to the common and threw his ball around for him for a while. He seemed as enthusiastic as ever, unaffected by his eviction. He chased the ball as though his life depended on it, leapt high for it, even headed it at times. He shook it and chewed it and, now and then, reluctantly let go of it for me to throw it again.

Later we lay in the long grass and I gazed up at the sky and wondered once more about that kitten. Then it rained.

By the time we reached the house, both of us were soaked. A squally wind whipped at the trees, rain bounced up from the slabs. For some reason I did not rush inside but went round the back and looked in through the kitchen window. Rain streamed down the glass, distorting the scene, but you could see enough. The kitten was on the table, motionless. Mum, Dad and Josie were grouped around it, their faces so solemn, tear-stained even, but that was probably the rain. Only Luke in his high chair seemed cheerful, banging his spoon.

Their faces so solemn

And the kitten again, just sitting there—like royalty.

Billy, meanwhile, was getting his view of things through the French window. He placed a sodden paw on the glass, tilted his head and whined. And that was odd too; Billy never whined.

The next day I tried talking to Mum.

"Mum, I've been thinking—this kitten, it's always eating."

Mum was removing a huge baked ham from the oven. "It's a growing cat—hand me that fork."

The gorgeous aroma of ham filled the kitchen.

"Who's that for?"

"Us."

"And it, I'll bet."

The kitten—cat—was elsewhere, in the sitting room probably, where it preferred to be, with the curtains closed (it had "sensitive eyes," according to Dad) and the TV on.

I decided to try a different approach. "I've been sneezing a lot."

"Oh, yes." Mum was carving the ham.

"And I think I'm getting a rash—it's that cat."

Mum paused and turned wearily toward me. "David, stop—"

"We should get rid of it!"

It was then, I think, that the first real wave of fear washed over me. What was happening to us?

Mum took little notice. It occurred to

me that she was still in her dressing gown, hair unbrushed, and it was lunchtime. Worse still, I thought I could detect in the air around her the faintest hint of cigarette smoke.

My parents were changing. Of course, to appreciate just how much, you need to know what they were like before. Well, normally, my dad was . . . normal: a neat dresser, collar and tie and all that, clean-shaven, punctual. He seemed to enjoy being a librarian. He was a "good" dad, took us out on our bikes, took us for pizzas, planned holidays.

Mum was the same, rushing home from her teaching job (part-time because of Luke), cooking for us, washing for us. She was secretary of the Lorries Campaign, a great jumble-sale organizer, and she was reliable. That was it, *reliable* (they both were), and talkative, nosy really, always wanting to know what you were up to. And both of them *loved* Billy.

Whereas now there wasn't much talking, even among themselves, the bikes went nowhere, Dad looked quite scruffy at times and Mum was smoking again.

With Josie, the changes were less obvious. She always did go in for scowling and sucking her thumb—when she was tired, according to Mum, when she wasn't getting her own way, I'd have said. Too much TV could send her into a hot and grumpy trance. But she was also funny and full of beans, always wanting her

friends round, forever after my PlayStation. She'd come down the stairs like a ton of bricks, eat three bowls of Frosties in a blink — and *she* loved Billy.

I tried talking to her.

About the PlayStation: "Fancy a game?"

"I dunno."

About her little pals: "How's Olivia?"

"I dunno."

Even about that kitten: "So what d'you think we should call it?"

Pause. Thumb out. And this from the girl who had a name for everything.

". . . I dunno."

The kitten for its part was still growing. (I may call it a cat from here on.) It was almost as big as a Labrador. Most of the time it skulked around in the sitting room. Occasionally it would squeeze under one of the beds upstairs. Once I found it on the landing.

I was coming out of my room and there it was, stretched out. I nearly fell over it. Its fur, I thought, was darkening, less gray now than black. Its yellow eyes stared up at me, fixed me. It did not move.

All cats have a coldness in their eyes, don't they? A remoteness, an absence of

feeling. But then cats, real cats, can't help
it. Whereas with this one you felt there was
something deliberate in its gaze, as though
it knew what it was up to.

It looked at me, I looked at it. A kind of
contest developed; which one of us would
look away? I found myself crouching
down, leaning forward. It seemed to be getting darker on the landing. The cat still held
my gaze . . . I put out a hand.

Just then there was a screech of brakes
out in the street, followed by angry voices.
(The lorries again.) I jumped to my feet
and glanced out of the window at the
hopping-mad couple on the pavement. I
went downstairs.

4

Proving It to George

"HOW BIG IS IT now?"

"As big as Flossie."

George smiled in disbelief.

"No, really, it is."

He and I were in the paddock playing dog football: me and Billy, supposedly, versus Flossie (Labrador), Spy (spaniel), Archie (indescribable) and George. The permanently deflated ball flew here and there, whenever one of us could get a kick at it, with the dogs in joyful pursuit.

"And it's Spy now, and he's got the ball
. . . and he's got the ball . . . and he's still got
the ball."

"Here's Billy—go on, Billy, tackle him!"

"Foul!"

"Hey, ref, send him off!"

"He's eating the ball. . . ."

Out on the "touchline" an ill-tempered

goose was hissing loudly. Donkeys wandered dreamily onto the pitch. The score remained nil–nil.

Eventually, worn out, we trailed back to the house. The dogs drank noisily from a trough in the yard. George and I sat in the kitchen with Alma.

I liked Alma. She was easygoing and eccentric. (George and I got parsnip wine sometimes with our homemade, wholemeal, low-fat, *organic* vegetarian pizza.) She took good care of her menagerie, which was constantly changing. It must have been hard work, yet she always had time for people. She was—what's the word?—yes, she was "hospitable."

"Alma, can cats hypnotize you?"

"No," said George.

"Yes," said Alma. She had a puppy on her lap and was feeding it warm milk with an eyedropper. "Especially Siamese." She lowered the puppy into a basket and picked up another. "Is this that cat of yours?"

"Yes . . . sort of."

"How big is it now?"

"This big—bigger than Flossie."

"You only said as big as Flossie before," said George. He had a puppy too.

Alma laughed. "Ah, yes, but it's probably grown since then."

"It has!" I felt myself smiling and scowling at the same time. "It's not funny."

Alma handed me her puppy and reached for another.

I told her about Billy and his removal to the garage.

"Poor Billy—what did he do?"

"Chased that bloody cat."

"*Bad* Billy."

Billy, hearing his name, glanced up at us from under the table, then returned his attention to the bone he was grappling with. (Billy liked Alma too.) I gazed down at the puppy cupped in my hands, its tiny gesturing paws, eyes still tightly shut and innocent bulging belly, smooth as a grape.

In the afternoon I went home and took George with me. I was determined he should see things for himself. George Riley was my best friend, but he could be irritating at times. He had an opinion on everything, especially subjects he knew nothing about. Because of his height, he

 was often assumed
by grown-ups to be
older than he was.
They credited him
with good sense and
maturity. That was especially irritating.

When we got to the house, Mum was in
the kitchen cooking a load of fish. There
were shopping bags, empty cartons, plastic
bottles all over the floor. Luke was in his
high chair, howling. No sign of Josie.

"Afternoon, Mrs. Burrell," said George,
maturely.

Mum mumbled something in reply.

I gave Lukey a kiss on his hot little
head and retrieved his panda from the
floor.

George and I stepped into the hall. The

smell of fish followed us, mingling soon with the disinfected odor of litter trays from the washroom. There was a pile of shoes near the front door, a scatter of envelopes and free newspapers on the mat, a couple of ice cream wrappers, an apple core. There were umbrellas and tennis rackets, even a small spade. I saw my home then through George's eyes. It was a tip. There again, given what he was accustomed to, it probably looked pretty tidy. And the smell would not have bothered him either.

I opened the sitting room door. The curtains were closed, the TV on, but the room was empty. We climbed the stairs . . . and there it was, on the landing again.

"There it is!"

"Where?"

He was expecting a "cat"

George's eyes were still adjusting to the gloom.

"See it?"

"I can't."

"There . . . Sh! . . . stretched out."

Still George couldn't see it. (Of course, he was expecting a "cat.")

And then he could.

"Christ!"

5

We Like This Better

HOW CURIOUS, COMICAL EVEN. I mean, here was I worried sick about this creature, its monstrous size, malignant presence, yet when George said, "Christ," and fell back in astonishment, I was actually pleased. That had shown him.

We sat out in the garden.

"That's not a cat."

"I *told* you."

"Not a normal cat."

"I know! Here, wait a minute."

I returned to the house. Josie was carrying a huge plate of steaming fish out of the kitchen.

"Hi, Josie."

No reply.

Mum was getting Luke into his buggy. The phone was ringing. I grabbed a photograph from the table and went out again.

"Here, look at this!"

It was a Polaroid taken the day of Josie's party. There was Josie on the patio, crouching, laughing, and there was the kitten—in a flowerpot.

"See—and it's got to this size in less than ten days."

"Weird," said George.

"Yes."

"Unscientific."

Nothing, in George's expert opinion, could grow that fast. Nothing normal.

"Then there's the other thing. I can't explain it, but it seems to have this . . . influence."

"Like hypnosis, y'mean."

"Yes, you saw Mum—she's like a zombie sometimes. Dad—you know what he's like—Dad went to work yesterday without a shave. And the day before he didn't go at all. As for Josie, well . . ."

"So there's only Luke who's normal," said George.

"Yes, and me."

"You're not normal." George gave me a shove.

I considered this for a moment, and jumped on him.

George left soon after for his trombone lesson. I went and sat with Billy in the garage. The up-and-over door was open. A stiff breeze ruffled Billy's fur. He was stretched out on his bit of blanket, still gnawing on that bone that Alma had given him. He had carried it all the way home. It was filthy now, covered in grass and dirt, but for Billy, I'll bet, it was absolute caviar. He growled if I went anywhere near it. So I sat watching Billy with his bone, and thinking. Only Luke was unaffected, and me. Why was that? I could hear the phone ringing in the house, unanswered. I pictured Josie's laughing face in the photograph,

Some kind of game show

that whole gang of little girls going mad in the garden. Now look at her. Only Lukey, only me. I stretched my legs out. Billy growled. Oh, yes—and Billy.

Later I went looking for Josie and found her in the sitting room. The TV was on, some kind of game show. A man and a woman were rushing around in a D.I.Y. store with a trolley. Josie was on the floor, thumb in her mouth, leaning back against the sofa, on which the cat was sitting. It was dark and stuffy in the room. There were bits of fish on the carpet.

I perched myself on the arm of a chair.

"Josie?"

She looked up.

"Fancy a game?"

(I had in mind the PlayStation, but it

could have been anything.)

Thumb out—"No . . . thanks"—and in again.

I reached for the remote control and flipped the channels: snooker—old movie—cartoon.

"Hey—look! I used to watch this."

Josie roused herself, snatched the remote from my hand and put the game show back on.

"We like this better," she said.

We like this better. I realize now I should have told more people, and sooner. But, as it happened, this was the holiday fortnight in our town. Most of the big employers, the shoe factory, the bicycle works, were shut down. Grandma, Grandpa, Uncle Mark

and his family, the Fletchers next door —
half the town, really, were away on holiday.
Anyway, in those early stages what could I
have said, and who would have believed
me? I was scared of a kitten.

The cat was staring at me, swishing its
tail. It wanted me out of there, I could feel
it. Well, tough. This was my house, my TV,
my sister (I slid down into the chair), and
I was staying where I was. The time for
keeping clear of this animal was over. Now,
if anything, I had to get closer to it, study it.
By this means and with George's help, I
might discover then how best, one way or
another, to get rid of it.

6

Cat Servants

W E CRUSHED UP THE tablets in George's bedroom. Paracetamol, tranquilizers, y'know, anything that warned of "drowsiness if taken in excess," all plundered from our bathroom cabinets or Alma's vet's cupboard. George spooned the powder into a plastic bag. "That ought to do it."

The plan was to mix this lot up in the cat's food, wait until it fell asleep, heave

it into a sack or bin
liner, load it onto one
of our bikes and
carry it away.
Where to exactly,
we had not decided,
but over the river most likely, up beyond
Addison's Farm. Anyway, wherever it was,
we meant to lose this cat completely. Yes,
"lose" it, and *across* the river, not into it. No,
not weighted down with rocks and such,
tied up in the sack. Not drowned. We never
thought of that.

Meanwhile, I was now watching the cat
whenever I got the chance, studying it,
stalking it (and *not* sneezing). Its favorite
places were the sitting room and under-
neath Mum and Dad's bed, the only one

 it could still get under. It came into the kitchen too, mostly to watch its food being prepared. It ate in the sitting room. It never went out.

The cat's feeding habits were crazy. (What was it costing us?) It ate huge meals five or six times a day—and night. Mum was up all hours cooking. There were lamb chops now, spaghetti Bolognese, puddings! One time I came into the kitchen and there was Dad pouring a whole pot of tea into a bowl for it, adding milk and sugar, while the cat sat back and waited.

Truth is, all three of them were attending

to this creature—feeding it, petting it, keeping it company—twenty-four hours a day. *They were its servants.* Mum "talked" to it more than she did to me. Josie seemed often to know what it was thinking. None of them, apparently, saw anything strange in what was happening. All my protests were ignored. Eventually I gave up making them.

And the house was becoming darker. At first I thought it was just the curtains, more of which were permanently closed. Later I began to suspect the cat. A room was gloomier when the cat was in it, and the longer it stayed the gloomier the room became. The air itself felt thicker and more stifling then. A kind of gauze hung over things.

As if all this were not enough, from following the cat around, observing it, I now felt pretty sure of something else: its *shape* was changing.

On Thursday, the day after we had crushed the tablets, I rang George and whispered down the phone.

"I've done it."

"Who's that?"

"Me—Davy. I've mixed it all in. It's ate the lot!"

There was a pause. George was turning his radio down.

"Brilliant—where is it now?"

"The sitting room."

"Is it, er . . ."

"No, but it soon will be. Come on round."

"Right."

"Fast as you can."

"Right."

"Oh, and George?"

"Yeah?"

I cupped my hand over the phone. Josie was descending the stairs.

"Bring the sack."

That morning (by eight o'clock!) Mum had produced this huge mixing bowl of stew for the cat. It had everything in it: minced beef, potatoes, carrots, onions, baked beans, leftover spaghetti, fish heads and masses of garlic. While her back was turned, I stirred my little contribution in, just for the flavor.

By the time George arrived, tapping on the French windows, Mum had driven off with Luke and Josie; shopping again, for the almost daily car-bootful. (What did Waitrose make of it?) George had with him his bicycle pump, some string and one of Alma's horse-feed sacks.

I led the way into the hall. We peeped through the crack in the sitting room door. The TV was on—it was never off these days—and the cat was there, staring at it.

"It doesn't *look* sleepy." George was fiddling with his string.

"Give it time."

"Yeah."

The trouble was, there was no time, or not much. We had to finish this before Mum came back.

"Let's go in there," said George.

The cat was on the sofa as usual, watching a gardening program. We stood there for a time, sneaking sideways glances at it, while it paid us no heed at all. The air was thick with the smell of stew. Unwashed bowls and plates littered the floor, a sock of Josie's, a tennis racket, cigarette ends.

I felt a sudden sense of desperation. This wasn't working at all. That cat could swallow a ton of pills, I bet, and not be affected. Meanwhile, the pink-cheeked, cheerful gardener went on about his aubergines, and the room grew darker.

The doorbell rang, though we hardly heard it. The room was closing in around us, its shapes dissolving, the television sound all muffled, indistinct. Only the glowing screen, the silhouetted cat, looked real. The doorbell rang again, and now there was loud knocking at the door, and voices.

I went into the hall. On the doorstep stood old Mrs. Rutter, her daughter and the twins.

"Is y'mother in?"

"No."

"Did she say anything about the leaflets?"

"No."

"Leave a box or anything?"

I shook my head.

Mrs. Rutter tutted and turned angrily to her daughter. "I dunno—what can y'do?"

Mrs. Rutter's daughter sighed. The

twins stirred fretfully in their buggy.

"Tell y'mother Mrs. Rutter called," said Mrs. Rutter.

"I will."

"Tell her we need those leaflets."

"Yes."

"*Also,* whenever she can't get to a meeting, tell her, could she please—"

"Mother!"

"Shurrup, it needs saying. Could she please let-other-people-know."

"I'll tell her that."

I began to close the door.

"Calls herself the bloomin' secretary."

"Mother!"

I hurried back into the sitting room. It was darker than ever; even the TV was shrouded over. The indistinct gray shape of the cat still occupied the sofa, but now there was George beside it. The air was stifling. Sweat broke out all over me. I felt a buzzing in my ears, a tight band across my chest. George was reaching for the cat. A pale hand in the gloom, stretching, hovering.

I had to speak, but couldn't. The solid air stuck in my throat. The TV picture quivered like a mirage. I moved, trod on and smashed a dirty plate, and spoke at last.

"Don't touch it!"

7

Panthers and All That

IT WAS THE STROKING. Somehow, all in a rush and grabbing George and pulling him away, I worked it out. I never stroked it, Luke never stroked it, Billy couldn't stroke it. But the others . . . I could see again that rain-streaked window, the cat on the table, Mum, Dad and Josie gathered round, their faces blank, their hands outstretched. Yes, the others stroked it all the time. They were addicted.

George and I stood in the kitchen, bright sunlight bouncing from the worktops, birdsong through the open window. It was hot and I was shivering.

"What were you doing? You were going to stroke it, weren't you?"

"Don't remember." George looked dazed. "It was getting so dark in there."

"Never stroke it, George, never. That's how—"

There was the sound of a car in the drive, doors slamming. Seconds later, in came Mum with Luke and Josie.

"Morning, Mrs. Burrell," said George.

"Hallo, er . . ." Mum gazed distractedly around the kitchen. "Er . . ."

"George," said George.

We helped to unload the car, bags and

bags of stuff, enough for a siege. Billy was barking and leaping around in the garage. Josie had disappeared.

I wanted to talk to Mum, but it was hopeless. No sooner were the bags unpacked than there she was cooking again. Besides, she looked so sad, so bewildered, I hadn't the heart to argue with her. George and I played with Luke for a while, entertained him in his bouncer, ate a couple of doughnuts and left.

And then—how comical again—out in the normal street with its normal noise and smells, the little normal kids in their push-chairs, normal Billy tugging on his normal lead, it all felt so . . . confusing. For a minute I hardly knew what to believe. Then, "It's changing its shape, I hope y'know,"

George said, and we were back into it.

On the way to Alma's we talked about the shape of the cat. There was something about its head and shoulders, the way it sat on the sofa, not catlike, almost human. We talked about the stroking, how one defenseless kitten might take control of people through its fur, just by getting them to stroke it. There again, who'd need persuading? Stroke a cat? I mean, it's the most natural thing in the world.

What we did not talk about, as far as I remember, was what this cat, this creature, actually *was*. What it was up to, where it had come from and so on. Later, when it was all over and the papers were full of theories (panthers and all that), we did. But at the time, no. Looking back, I think somehow it just crept up on us, so to speak, shifting its ground so gradually, step by step, that, mad as it seems, we took it for granted.

At Alma's they were playing dog tennis in the paddock. Alma and Joyce, each with a racket, were batting tennis balls back and forth, which the dogs, like crazy ball boys, were intercepting. It was the usual gang: Archie, Flossie, Spy, plus on this occasion an elderly bulldog named Jasper, who was Joyce's, and one newcomer, a lolloping Saint Bernard.

"Who's this?" said George.

"That's Winston," said Alma. "Here on a visit."

Meanwhile, Billy was off his lead and into the game. The other dogs were effective in their various ways, but Billy was the star, and he knew it. Archie could chase, Spy was crafty, even lumbering Jasper had his moments—but Billy! He was so quick—so

springy—so fearless. He'd leap and catch the ball in midair, and fall, and bounce (just like a ball himself), and not let go.

Later, we tried talking to Alma again about the cat. It wasn't easy. Somehow when you put a thing like this into words, it can sound absurd, y'know, especially with someone like Alma.

"It never goes out, Mum," said George. "Never purrs—never washes itself."

Alma laughed. "Neither do you, half the time."

George pressed on. "And it really is huge—gets bigger every time you see it."

Alma was slicing a loaf and making sandwiches.

She turned to me. "Hm—what does y'mum and dad say?"

"Dad says it's the breed."

"Hm . . . pass me that lettuce."

On the floor in the corner, the puppies were scrabbling around in their box.

"Tell her about the stroking," said George.

"Right." I took a deep breath. "See, it's . . ."

Alma handed me a plate.

"It's, well . . ."

She put aside her knife and gave me her full attention.

"It's . . ."

"You stroke it," said George, "and it gets this power over you."

"Ah," said Alma.

At this point in came Joyce, holding a pigeon.

"Tell Joyce," said Alma.

Joyce sat with the pigeon on her lap, smoothing its feathers with her finger. Alma poured her a cup of tea.

"Tell Joyce what?" said Joyce.

Talking to Alma was tricky; talking to Alma and Joyce, plus a pigeon, half a dozen puppies and a braying donkey at the window, was near enough impossible. By the time I left, the jokes were flying again and we were no further forward.

That evening I sat in my room and stared out of the window. Billy—I had sneaked him in—was sleeping on the bed beside me. Golden light lay flat across the patchwork of gardens, a fading vapor trail stretched out above the houses, shadows lengthened.

Earlier I had told Mum about Mrs. Rutter and offered to take the lorry leaflets round to her house. But of course there were no leaflets; she had failed to get them printed. At teatime Suzannah and her mum stopped by, inviting Josie to go on a trip and sleep over. Josie merely scowled (this

That evening I sat in my room

was probably her best friend), while Mum stood in the doorway saying little and not inviting them in.

When Dad came home, I took a chance and tried to get some camp money out of him. I needed it, I explained, to buy a torch plus a few other things. I showed him the list the school had provided. Dad looked really wild. His hair was all over the place and I thought he was going to yell at me. Instead he gave me twenty pounds!

I lay on the bed and stared at the ceiling. I was, I suppose, a natural pessimist (still am!); a boy who feared the worst and worried about it, but in this case my worries were doubled. After all, what exactly was the worst? The situation was forever shifting. The cat got bigger, the problem got bigger;

its shape changed, the problem changed. I could not hold it steady in my mind. At times it felt like I was going mad. This business with a huge hypnotic cat was unbelievable. I know what I said earlier, about taking the cat for granted and all that, but this was the truth too. Truths and contradictions, yes, in those days my head was full of them. (Still is!)

From the sitting room there came a sudden burst of TV laughter. Luke was asleep in the room next to mine. (I had looked in on him.) But the others, they were down there, weren't they? Feeding it, stroking it, *serving it*. And there'd be no light on, just the TV and a candle sometimes. And the curtains closed. And a thickening, sickening darkness. Unbelievable.

Beside me on the bed, Billy stirred. A soft growl fluttered in his throat and his paws twitched. I rubbed the coarse fur along his back and stroked his ears. Good old Billy . . . he'd believe it.

8

Shopping

I NEVER SHOULD HAVE gone on the camp. I never meant to, at least that's what I told myself. Whereas the truth is (truths and contradictions again), I wanted to go more than anything. To escape—yes, that's it. To escape the mess and the smell, the peculiar gathering gloom in the house, the pitiful look in my mother's eyes, the responsibility. After all, it was only five days, and it was paid for. Gran and

Grandpa would be home when I returned, and Uncle Mark and Auntie Alison. I could tell them and they could sort it out.

George had other ideas. (It was easier for him, he wasn't living with it.) He thought we should switch to plan B. Apart from wearing gloves, however, it turned out he had no idea what plan B was. The cat was now too big to handle. We could have picked it up between us and carried it, probably, but not far, and not at all unless it wanted us to. I mean, just viewed simply as a cat, it was a dangerous creature.

I should say something here about the camp. Once a year, usually at the end of August, one of the teachers, Mr. Thomas, and his wife took a party of children to Devon. His dad had a farm there and we camped in one of his fields. George and I had been before.

In the next couple of days my conscience worked overtime. Getting my things together—rucksack, sleeping bag, et cetera—ticking stuff off on my list, was a guilty pleasure. Meanwhile, I was avoiding the cat again, afraid of what I would see. And helping Mum (more guilt), loading the dishwasher, tidying my room. Dad was off work quite often now, getting up late, drifting around in the garden with his hands in his pockets. I helped him too; pulled some weeds out, washed the car.

On Friday I went shopping with Mum and Luke. Mum, I have since realized, no longer trusted herself to drive; she smoked almost continuously and her hands

shook. We walked and pushed Luke's buggy to the corner shop.

Side by side with my mother on the street, I felt embarrassed. She looked so odd, y'know, pale and haunted, and thin. (All that cooking and she was hardly eating, none of them were.) Her hair was untidy, her lipstick smeared. I felt people staring at us. As we entered the shop, we met a suntanned Mrs. Fletcher coming out. I could see the startled look on her face, but before much was said, Mum had bundled us inside.

Pardoes' was a curious shop, a small door and window at the front and a great long windowless aisle at the back. The Pardoes had owned and run it for years. It sold pretty well everything.

Mum moved rapidly and anxiously along the shelves, muttering to herself as she went. Whenever I fell behind (there were a couple of things I needed), she urged me on. We had to hurry up, she said, yes, hurry up. Not keep him waiting. I did not think she meant my dad.

And what was she buying? A load of liver, a shoulder of lamb, frankfurters and other sausages, smoked haddock, pickles, gherkins, mustard, olives, a huge amount of pasta, a dozen tins of anchovies, three large tubs of tuna pâté . . .

The trolley was almost full; Luke perched upon a mountain of food. (How would we carry it?) Mum added a bottle of wine and then another. Finally, as I watched in horror, she took a small flat bottle of vodka down from a shelf and slipped it into Luke's nappy bag. The smile she gave me, when I caught her eye, was crafty and ashamed.

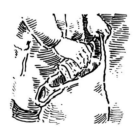

9

Thomas's Farm

THE FOLLOWING MORNING AT half-past six I sat on the coach with George and Kenny Biggs. As we pulled away, a crowd of sleepy-eyed parents cheered and waved. Alma and Joyce (with Jasper) were there, and my dad, standing apart, his hand in an anxious gesture to his mouth, not waving.

So the coach took us away. Away from the school and the street and the town.

Away from our parents, brothers, sisters, pets. Away from our comfy beds and familiar breakfasts, computer games and favorite TV programs. Away from everything.

Thomas's Farm was a brilliant place, halfway up a hill. It had cornfields and an orchard. There was a stable block where local riders kept their ponies and horses. There were pigs and chickens and calves, trees to climb, ropes to swing on and a cockerel to wake you up in the morning.

I liked the calves best, and my favorite job was feeding them. Most people think cows feed calves, but they don't, though I'm not sure why. What happens is, you take this bucket of milk, dip your finger into it and the calf just comes along and sucks it. Gradually you bring your finger closer to the surface of the milk until the calf is drinking straight from the bucket. As simple as that.

Well, we arrived and pitched our tents and got the Calor gas cookers going and spread our groundsheets and listened to a speech from old Mr. Thomas—what *not* to do—and went for a walk (to tire us out, which never worked) and ate and drank . . . and didn't sleep.

That night our torches flashed forever in the darkness. When morning came, I reckon we woke the cockerel up.

If this was some other story (which I wish to God it was), I could write lots of stuff about that camp, pages and pages. The delicious food for a start: burnt-black

sausages and beans, the freshest eggs,
straight from the hen. And the trips we
went on—the encounters we had with kids
from the village—the bonfire and singing
on the last night—foxes and owls,
romances, melodramas, ghosts.

As it is, well, I had fun, I can't deny it.
I was distracted. I forgot, though not for

long and never entirely. The scene in Pardoes' shop kept coming back to me; the cat lurked always at the edges of my mind.

On the afternoon of the third day, the five of us from our tent, me, George, Kenny and the Crossley twins, were helping to stack some bales of straw in the top field. It was hot and scratchy work with little scope for fooling around until Mr. Thomas left us for a while.

Soon we had created a staircase with the bales and after that a den. There was much racing around and wrestling. Eventually, pink-faced and smothered in straw dust, we lay out on the cropped field and caught our breath. It was then, staring up into the dazzling sky, the spiky ground

beneath me like a bed of nails, that I got
the idea, the cat idea. It was so obvious, so
simple. Why hadn't I thought of it before?
It was the natural solution. I told George.

"What y'whisperin' about?" said Alex.

"Nothing," said George.

"We could *do* it," I said.

"Do what?" said Kenny.

"It's a secret," said George.

"What is?" said Darren.

"It would *work*," I said.

"What would?" said Alex.

". . . Yes," said George.

That night I lay in my sleeping bag
feeling much better than I had, less guilty,
less ashamed. There was something to do
now, details to be worked out, plan B.
As I drifted into sleep, the others already

asleep, odd thoughts and memories flickered in my mind. George had got himself a girl-friend, Imogen Hobbs, though both of them denied it. I pictured my mother, her shaky efforts to pack my bag, make my sandwiches, slipping me extra pocket money as I left the house. I had not told George about the vodka. The girls had seen a ghost down by the stables, something about a face in a tree. My mother was no thief. George and Imogen . . .

Rain fell softly on the shadowy canvas.

. . . It would work.

10

Coming Home

ON THURSDAY AT HALF-PAST eight
we arrived back at the school. Heavy
cloud obscured the evening light. Rain had
recently fallen and some of the parents still
had their umbrellas up.

There was no one to meet me (the
coach was a bit early), so I got a lift with
Alma and George. As we drove along,
Alma interrogated us in her cheerful
way. She gazed lovingly into George's

face and wondered aloud if he had used his soap or even unwrapped it. When we reached the house, our car was just visible in the drive and the front door of the house was ajar. I heaved my things out of the boot and waved to Alma as she drove off.

What I saw first was the gatepost, snapped off and splintered on the drive. The car had a massive dent in its bonnet; the front bumper was hanging loose. What I heard first was Billy.

I dropped my rucksack and ran. Billy was leaping about on his long lead, overjoyed to see me — he nearly

took off. His food bowl was empty—licked clean—his water bowl nearly empty. A sack of jumble that he appeared to have attacked was scattered in rags around the garage. There was a revolting smell of dog shit.

In a mad rage, hating my family at that moment, I ran to the kitchen. The blinds were down, the lights wouldn't work, there was rubbish and mess everywhere.

"Dad?"

"Mum?"

No answer.

I opened a tin of Pal for Billy, rushed out with it and rushed back again.

"Dad?"

No answer.

I stepped into the hall.

"Mum?"

Upstairs I could hear music playing, voices. It was so dark, even in the hall, even with the door open. I got the torch out of my rucksack and climbed the stairs.

There was a radio playing in my parents' room.

"Mum . . . Dad . . ."

I switched it off and shone my flickering torch around. The room was hardly recognizable. The bed had been upended against the wall and the mattress was on the floor. Cups and plates and chicken bones littered the floor. A blanket had been nailed across the window. It wasn't a bedroom anymore, y'know? It was a den.

I looked in Josie's room, and Luke's. Nothing. With a thumping heart, I

I could hear music playing

descended the stairs and stood again in the hall. Billy was still barking in the garage. A car alarm was sounding down the street. No sound at all came from the sitting room. I opened the door.

A wall of hot, foul, smoky air hit me in the face. I was immediately bathed in sweat.

"Mum . . . Josie . . ."

The darkness in the room was almost solid. I felt like I was wading through it, slowly, slowly. Three or four candles glimmered faintly on the mantelpiece and dresser. The TV was on but without the sound.

It took me an age to cross the room. The easy chair had been moved. It was in front of the TV now with its back to the door. A small table stood beside it. There was a wineglass, I could see, a plate of food,

 a smoldering cigar. The cat, or rather what the cat had become, was sitting upright in the chair. It turned its fearsome head and gazed at me with no concern at all. The sound that came from me then — a groan? a scream? — was terrifying in itself. The torch fell from my fingers. I saw the cat raise the wineglass to its lips . . . and ran.

I was out in the street, panic still rising in my throat, my thoughts in turmoil, frantic. Soft, steady rain was falling from a gray sky. A car went past, its headlights gleaming. I ran to the Fletchers' house — rang the bell — banged on the door — banged on the window. No one came. I stood in their porch, out of the rain, shivering. A lorry trundled loudly down the street. Another car. A motorbike.

I struggled then to organize my thoughts. What had I *seen*? (I'd run before there was time to see.) The size of it? The shape of it? A gleam of eyes and teeth. What else? The strangeness of its posture, the empty, alien look it gave me. The wineglass.

My heart was pounding less. I pushed the wet hair from my eyes and wondered what to do. Where were they? Shopping again, all four of them, at this hour? Pardoes' hardly ever shut; perhaps that was it. I could go there—now—meet them. But then what? Whatever I said, they'd take no notice, just carry on as before, like robots.

I could go to Grandma's, catch a bus to Uncle Mark's. But I had no money. The money was in my rucksack . . . in the house. I could go to George's.

Something came brushing against my leg in the gloom—"Ah!" It was only the Fletchers' cat, though, bedraggled and miaowing, hoping the door would open. I resisted the urge to boot it off the porch.

I went to George's.

11

Not Much Longer Now

HALF AN HOUR LATER I was back in the house, sweating like mad again and yelling at Dad. I had found him in the kitchen, a frown on his face, a beard on his face, surrounded by Pardoes' bags. The worktop lights were on, throwing deep shadows down the room. Flies buzzed noisily over the plates of half-eaten, half-rotten food that covered the table. There was a persistent stench of sour milk.

"Where *were* you?" I launched straight in, all else for those few seconds forgotten.

"Er . . ." Dad gestured vaguely at the piles of shopping. He had a bottle of sherry in his hand that he was pouring into a cup.

"You never met me — I had to get a lift with Alma!"

"Oh . . ." He took a swig. "Sorry about that."

"And what about Billy?"

"He's all right."

"He's not all right. Y'never fed him — you feed that bloody thing!"

"Don't swear," said Dad, dully, automatically.

"Bloody thing. Y'never took him for walks. He's out there now—shit everywhere!"

"Don't say 'shit.'"

"Shit!" I shouted, as the anger (and fear and frustration) flooded through me. "It is shit, Dad. It's shitty! The whole thing, the whole business, the—"

Unexpectedly then, while wanting to say so much, I found myself unable to speak and burst into tears. Dad came over and put his hand, shyly almost, on my shoulder.

"Oh, Davy . . . don't." He patted me softly and drank his sherry. "Don't get upset. (Upset!) It'll be all right." His voice was low, his speech a little slurred. "It won't be for much longer now," I think I heard him say. And then the craziest remark: "Don't spoil things."

Don't spoil things. What did he *mean*? Spoil things! My rage boiled over again. (A useful rage, I later realized. It stoked my courage up, which I was going to need.) I yelled at Dad about the shopping. He was fiddling with the bags, lifting stuff out.

"No dog food, I'll bet!"

I challenged him about that creature.

"What is it in there—it's not a cat now, is it?"

Dad muttered something I couldn't hear. He had a hand up to his mouth, that anxious gesture. Tears shining now in *his* eyes.

There was a sound then in the hall behind me, a rising siren of howling baby.

Luke! I did not hes-
itate. If I had hesi-
tated, I would
never have moved.
I stumbled into the
hall. It was like a
tunnel in there,
black and smoky. A

tiny stain of light seeped out around the sitting room door. I shoved the door . . . and
saw them.

Mum had Luke in her arms, Josie
beside her. They were standing there, that's
all, just standing and watching the creature
in the chair, as it was watching the still-
silent TV.

What did I think? What horrifying
sacrifice did I assume? Or was it just that

Luke was there at all? Would it be his turn soon? It was the shifting situation again; I could not get my head round it. And what had Dad meant: "Not much longer now"? Was it leaving? Were there changes, transformations, still to come?

Well, I did not think, that's the truth of it. If I had, I would have got them out of there somehow and waited. As it was, I blundered forward, grabbed the first thing I could lay my hands on—a tennis racket—and brought it down with all my might upon the creature's head. Mum screamed and stepped away. But Josie, *Josie* came at me, furious anger in her face—"No!"—and grabbed my arm.

I pushed her aside and raised the racket again. It was no contest. I was

I sensed it towering over me

trying to attack a thing that frightened me so much I could not bear to look at it. I hit the back of the chair. The creature rose then to its feet, unhurt, it seemed. I sensed it towering over me, the swing of its misshapen arm.

I was flat on the floor, my ears ringing, a taste of blood in my mouth. Mum was beside me, helping me to my feet. Dad was in the doorway. He staggered forward, hurled his bottle at the creature's head and smashed the TV. Blue sparks danced where the screen had been. The noise now was tremendous, all of us yelling, screaming, crying. We huddled in a corner behind the sofa, while the cat — I forced myself to look — observed us.

The terror in that room was unbearable.

A sickening dizziness washed over me. I was about to faint away, when, airborne and like a bullet almost, in came Billy.

Thinking about it, years later, it's so obvious. This was always how it would end: cats and dogs, those ancient enemies, the natural solution. I remember how I'd laughed aloud at the neatness of it — my brain wave — there on that spiky, close-cropped field with George and the others, fooling around with the bales in the sunlight. For a dog will always see off a cat, won't it? And if one dog is not enough . . .

Billy came in as though off a ramp, flying. He was drenched, which made him look smaller than ever, but his courage was huge and unhesitating. He hit the cat, sank his teeth into its upper arm (while keeping up a constant growling) and hung on. Archie and Spy were close behind, snapping and leaping. Flossie, the oldest dog with the poorest eyesight, leapt and missed. Jasper, the slowest, walked in and grabbed an ankle. Winston had yet to arrive.

For a moment the advantage lay with the dogs. The cat twisted and turned to meet each new assault, unsure which one to deal with first. Then . . . Billy was hurled across the room, airborne once more, and hit the dresser. Hissing and spitting (catlike again), the cat knocked over the chair and caught poor Archie a terrible raking blow with its claws. Archie whimpered and retreated; Spy likewise. Jasper, the most fearsome growler of them all, hung on, shaking and tearing at the cat's ankle, his jaws clamped tight like a trap.

Winston arrived, slamming the cat so hard that it stumbled and fell. Even off-balance, it lashed out, catching the dog a savage swipe to the head. There was blood everywhere: Winston's, Archie's, the cat's. Flossie was on the floor, struggling to rise, her shoulder dislocated in an earlier attack, her leg broken. Meanwhile, a small fire had started. A stack of newspapers was smoldering in a corner, ignited by a fallen candle.

Billy came again. The confusion was unimaginable: smoke—flames—noise—

blood. Billy, though, I'd have to say, was not confused, never had been. This was still a cat, whatever its size or shape, and this was still his home, y'know, his *territory*. Yes, Billy had his reasons, twice over. Growling ferociously now, he darted in once more and seized the cat by its ear as it ducked and weaved, trying to get at Jasper. The cat reared up, snarling, while Billy dangled perilously, legs in air, like a ridiculous earring.

How slowly time moves, at times. All this, from start to finish, had happened in seconds. (George was still out on the drive!) Now, as I watched, the cat seized Billy with its razor teeth and tore his side wide open, and tossed him away.

A dog will always see off a cat, yes, but what if the cat is too strong? What if the dogs are torn and battered, and killed?

The cat *was* too strong. It had only to stand and fight to win. And yet. Maybe it was the light from the flames now leaping up. (Those sensitive eyes, remember?) Or Jasper's horrendous, bone-crunching grip, Spy's nonstop snapping and barking. Or the smoke. Or the absolute bedlam in that small room. Or . . .

The cat ran. It turned and leapt straight through the window, dragging the curtains with it, shattering the glass and the frame, freeing itself from Jasper at last. George, still steeling himself to enter the house, saw it all. The cat came flying out in a shower of splintering wood and glass. On all fours it bounded and flowed across the drive, smashed clean through the hedge . . . and was hit by a lorry.

12

Aftermath

THE CAT LAY CRUSHED and mangled, flattened between a giant tanker and the Co-op Bakery wall. Later the driver was to speak of his "unnerving experience." (I have the newspaper clipping here beside me.) An immense "cat" caught in the headlights, arriving from nowhere. The desperate application of the brakes, the screeching, the skidding, the unearthly scream-cum-roar of the animal itself, the thunderous collision with the wall, which was demolished.

The driver suffered a broken jaw. So, as a matter of fact, did Winston, who also lost an eye. That any of the dogs—the injured ones—survived at all was down to Alma. Even as the police and fire brigade were arriving, she drove up and with Joyce's help whisked them away. There was this vet Alma knew, had regular dealings with (a vet, as it happens, she later married).

The police had loads of questions, though what they made of our answers it's hard to say. From one small kitten in three short weeks, to this! They questioned George about his role in the affair (bringing the dogs, releasing Billy). And Alma too. George had told her nothing,

it seemed. She was simply out looking
for him.

Above all, I suppose, they wanted to
know what it *was*, and we couldn't tell them.
The evidence was unclear. What was eventually revealed, beneath the rubble, was the
pulverized body of a giant cat, but what sort
of cat? Some peculiarities in its shape were
discovered, but otherwise it was impossible
to be sure of anything.

*

We stood on the pavement with blankets around our shoulders watching the firemen put out the fire. The rain had stopped, a breeze was shifting the clouds away and layers of purple and pale green sky stretched out above the town. Dad had Josie in his arms, Mum had Luke, and I had Billy.

Billy, poor ruined Billy. His little corpse lay in my arms like a bloodstained rag. My guilty tears spilled out and splashed his head. I pressed my face into his fur and kissed him. Softly, from a long way down, Billy growled.

He wasn't dead; he was only ninety-nine percent dead. So Billy was rushed to the vet's too. And they stitched him up.

And bandaged him up. And fastened some kind of corset round him. And told us to keep him in cotton wool for a month.

And Billy lived.

*The fire did not destroy the house entirely, but we
moved anyway. We couldn't live there anymore,
it was impossible. And time does heal, doesn't it?
Yes, over the years our family has become a family
again. There's even one more of us now—Baby
Alice. Actually, the others—Mum, Dad, Josie—
recovered more quickly than I did. They were in
it, I guess you'd say, anesthetized by it. They saw
less, remembered less, dreamt less. Me? I was the
witness; I saw it all.*

*Anyway, that's it: end of cat, end of story.
Except . . . I do sometimes wonder what the
alternative ending might have been. If, say,
somehow we had left it alone, allowed it to . . .
develop. What size would it have stopped at,
what shape, what powers? (And I remember that
weird remark of Dad's: "Not much longer now.")*

There again, was it a one-off, really, a coin that stood on end, our share of strangeness? Or might there be others of its kind in the world, in other countries, cities, towns; miaowing and limping their way into other sunlit (or snowy) gardens?

Like yours, for instance.

About the Author

ALLAN AHLBERG has been writing children's books for twenty-five years. During this time he has produced many bestsellers, including *Each Peach Pear Plum* and *The Jolly Postman*. His recent work includes *The Adventures of Bert* (with Raymond Briggs) and *My Brother's Ghost*. Allan Ahlberg lives in England.

About the Illustrator

PETER BAILEY has illustrated books by many of the best-known writers for children, including Philip Pullman and Dick King-Smith. He lives near Liverpool with his wife, Siân, who is also an illustrator.